DATE DUE

Jafta—The Journey

Story by Hugh Lewin

Pictures by Lisa Kopper

🌱 Carolrhoda Books, Inc. / Minneapolis

Jafta—The Journey

Story by Hugh Lewin

Pictures by Lisa Kopper

🌿 Carolrhoda Books, Inc. / Minneapolis

I was so excited the day we went to town, said Jafta.
I had never been to town before,
and we were going to stay with my father,
who has to work there.

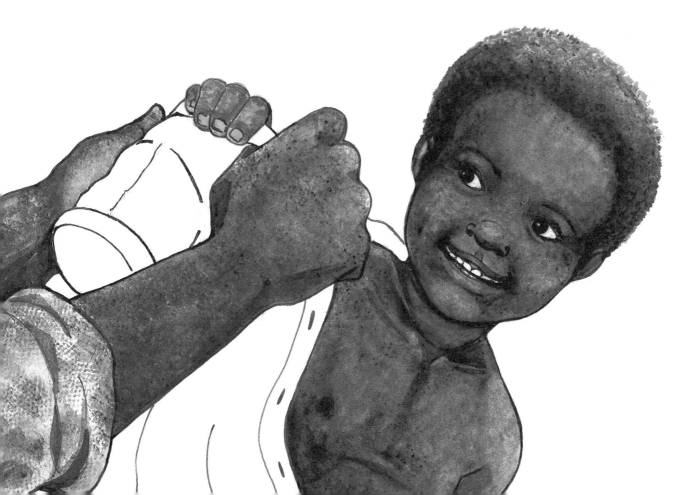

We were up long before the sun.
Mother cooked us tea and said, "Hurry, hurry, hurry.
We must reach Baba Caleb's store in time to catch the bus."
Uncle Josh helped us pack, and
just as the mountains began to light up,
we set off.

We walked through
three valleys before
reaching Baba Caleb's.

We stopped only once for water,
but twice Mother had to call
to Uncle Josh
because he kept talking
to the women in the fields.

My arms were beginning to ache when we arrived at the store where Baba Caleb was already getting his cart ready. I always like riding on the back of the cart, but today it was even more fun because it was piled high with driftwood and mealies.

I had never before been
beyond the first turnoff.
The road bumped down a hill
to a shallow ford where we could cross the river.
I jumped off and ran ahead.
Suddenly I heard Mother scream.
The cart had tilted and a wheel had fallen off.

"Oh, dear," cried Mother, "we mustn't miss the bus."
But Baba Caleb quickly calmed the oxen,
and we all helped jam rocks behind the other wheel.
Uncle Josh and Baba Caleb lifted the cart with a strong pole,
and Mother slid the wheel back on.

The sun was high when we reached the long, straight road. There we saw a crowd standing under a tree. Mother relaxed now and chatted happily with her friends. I was helping unload the cart when there was a deep growling from over the hill. The bus came toward us and stopped just where we were.

It was already very full,
but they piled more things on the roof,
and we were bundled in among legs
and arms and strange faces.
Then the bus bounced back
on to the road.
Uncle Josh waved us good-bye.

At other stops along the way the driver
managed to squeeze in more people
until we were so full
I could see nothing in front
except people and boxes and animals.
The fields outside rushed past
faster and faster.

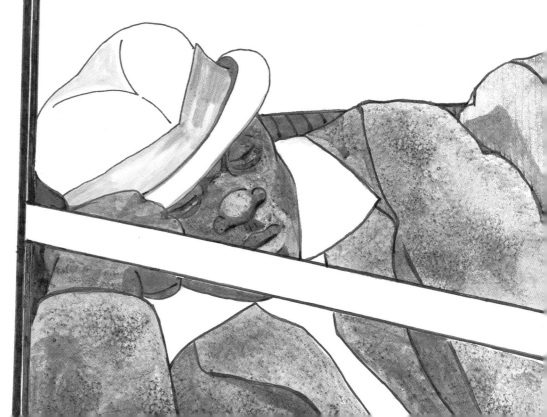

The best part of all
was when we reached the big river.
A large flatboat came toward us,
pulled by a line of singing men.

We had to climb out
as the bus drove slowly aboard.
The boat didn't sink,
even when we all walked on.
The men pulled us across the river.

I fell asleep on Mother's lap after that.
When I woke up, all I remember is that the sun had gone down
and there were lights and noise everywhere.
And there, among all the faces,
was my father, smiling
and reaching up for me.

For Josie

LIBRARY OF CONGRESS CATALOGING IN PUBLICATION DATA

Lewin, Hugh.
   Jafta — the journey.

   Summary: Jafta, a South African boy,
travels with his mother to the city where
his father works.
   [1. South Africa — Fiction. 2. Travel —
Fiction] I. Kopper, Lisa, ill. II. Title.
PZ7.L58418Jafs   1984   [E]   84-4326
ISBN 0-87614-265-X (lib. bdg.)

This edition first published 1984 by Carolrhoda Books, Inc.
Original edition published 1983 by Bell & Hyman, Publishers, London, England.
Text copyright © 1983 by Hugh Lewin.
Illustrations copyright © 1983 by Lisa Kopper.
All rights reserved.

Manufactured in the United States of America

4   5   6   7   8   9   10   93   92   91